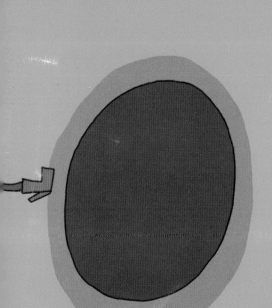

Key

 giant mud puddle

 hose = shower

 sheet = queen's robe
+ parachute
+ pirate's sash

 flowerpot = crown

 stick = scepter + sword

 tree house = airplane

 front porch = pirate ship

 board = pirate ship's plank

 pool = ocean full of
sea monsters

 girl + dog = best friends

For Lauren, who is an excellent imaginer
And for Meagster, who brings the fun

Dirt + Water = Mud
Copyright © 2016 by Katherine Hannigan
All rights reserved. Manufactured in China.
For information address HarperCollins Children's Books,
a division of HarperCollins Publishers
195 Broadway, New York, NY 10007
www.harpercollinschildrens.com

Adobe Photoshop, 140-pound Arches hot press watercolor paper,
and watercolor paints were used to create the full-color art.
The text of this book is set in Doctor Soos Light and Go Boom! Regular.

Library of Congress Cataloging-in-Publication Data is available.
ISBN 978-0-06-234517-2 (trade ed.)
16 17 18 19 20 SCP 10 9 8 7 6 5 4 3 2 1
First Edition
Greenwillow Books

Ah-roo-ooh-ooh!

(which means, Ho, ho, ho!)

Oh-roo!

$11 + 5 = 16$

(which means, Peek-a-boo!)

DIRT + WATER = MUD

Katherine Hannigan

Greenwillow Books
An Imprint of HarperCollins Publishers

DIRT + WATER = MUD

10, 9, 8, 7, 6, 5, 4, 3, 2, 1 . . .

MUD + SPLASH + SPLATTER =

VERY MUCKY

HOSE + HIGH UP = SHOWER

Come on.

Shhhhh.

SHEET + FLOWERPOT + STICK =

HER MAJESTY, THE QUEEN
(+ KNIGHT)

I hereby dub thee
Sir Licks-a-Lot.

Make way for the royal procession!

Hmm . . .

Uh-roo?

(which means, Where are you going?)

BLUE SKY + BREEZE : FLYING

Co-pilot, get on board.
The plane is taking off!

Ur-roo.

(which means, Hey . . .

Ur-roof.

I can't climb up there . . .

Ur-roof ROOF!

I'm down here all by myself . . .

UR-ROOF!

ROOF!
ROOF!
ROOF!

UR-ROOOOO!

And I don't want to be without you . . .   for one more second . . .   I miss you! Please come back to me!)

Sigh. . .

(which means, I am so lonely there are no words for it.)

TWO FRIENDS TOO FAR APART + SHEET =

PARACHUTE

Look out below!

Just one second.

SHEET + STICK + CAT'S EAR =

PIRATE
(+ FIRST MATE)

SHIP AHOY!

MEAN PIRATE + MAD FIRST MATE =

MUTINY!

Friend who's been splashed with mud + left on
the ground by a pilot + bossed around by a pirate =

not ready to forgive (yet)

Ar-roo!

(which means, Oh, no! . . .

Ar-roof-roof-ROOOOOF!

Hold on! I'm coming! I'll save you! . . .

Ar-roo?

Did I make it in time?)

Just . . . one . . .

second.

GIRL + DOG

+ PLAYING AND PRETENDING ALL DAY =

TWO BEST FRIENDS, ALL TIRED OUT ...

UNTIL TOMORROW.

Zzzzzzzz . . .
(which means, Good night.)